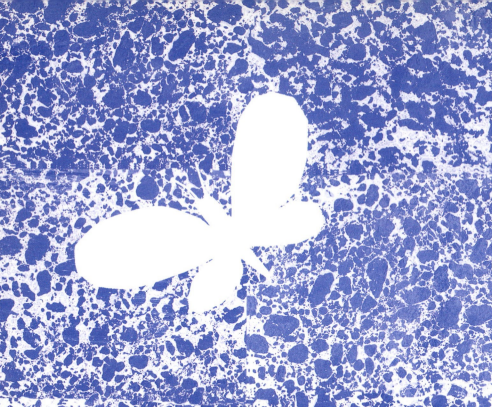

For all little ones who will let go of their moms
(and for all moms who manage to let go of their little ones)

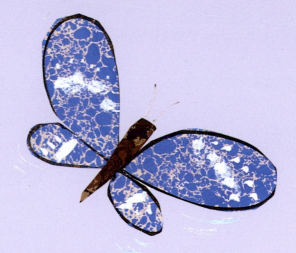

Little Kangaroo

Guido van Genechten

Clavis
NEW YORK

Mother Kangaroo had a problem.
That problem was sitting in her pouch.
It was big and heavy, but also very cute,
and it fiddled with her fur all day.

Little Kangaroo had become too big to be sitting in Mom's pouch.
It was about time, Mother Kangaroo thought,
for Little Kangaroo to hop through life on her own legs.

But Little Kangaroo didn't want that at all!
Mom's pouch was nice and soft.
Little Kangaroo got milk and a wash in it every day.
Moreover, a pouch like this was very useful:
she did not have to jump herself to get anywhere.

So every time that Mother Kangaroo
managed to push Little Kangaroo out of her pouch with a few kind words,

Little Kangaroo jumped – HOP! – back into it.

"The world is a lot bigger than my pouch,
and also much more beautiful," Mother Kangaroo said.
"Just look at how the butterflies fly through the air,
from flower to flower."
Little Kangaroo thought that butterflies were annoying
and didn't think much of flitting about.
No, she'd much rather stay with Mother Kangaroo.

"Look at how the elephants play in the water," Mother Kangaroo pointed out.
"Elephants are silly," said Little Kangaroo.
And the splash of water that landed on her nose, she found that silly as well.
At least it was warm and dry in Mom's pouch.

Mom tried again. "Just listen to the birds singing."
"I love to dance when I hear them. Don't you?"
"No, I don't," Little Kangaroo said firmly,
even though her left leg had been swinging
up and down the whole time.
She found the tweeting far too busy.
Little Kangaroo preferred to listen
to the noises in Mom's tummy.
They made her feel calm.

"Do you see how happy the monkeys are, swinging from tree to tree?"
Mother Kangaroo asked.
Little Kangaroo thought monkeys were funny,
but swinging in trees was surely dangerous.
Only in Mom's pouch did Little Kangaroo feel safe,
so that's where she stayed.

"Look at how joyfully the giraffes run across the plain," Mother Kangaroo said.

Little Kangaroo thought giraffes were great. How they could run!
But the plains were so vast that they made her dizzy.
She knew every little corner of Mom's pouch.

Finally Mother Kangaroo sat down, utterly exhausted.
All day long she had carried Little Kangaroo around in her pouch.
"More! More!" Little Kangaroo called out impatiently.
"I want to see everything!"
But Mother Kangaroo could not move another inch.

At that moment somebody came jumping towards them from a distance.
Little Kangaroo watched with big eyes.
These were the biggest, most beautiful jumps that she had ever seen!
The dust tickled her little nose when the jumper stopped right in front of her.

Little Kangaroo noticed that he looked like her.
He had the same nose, the same ears,
the same jumper's legs and a strong tail like her.
"Are you coming?" he asked.
"Yes, I am," said Little Kangaroo,
"if you teach me to jump just like you do."
And all of a sudden she jumped out of Mom's pouch…

… into the wide world.
To her great surprise, it was as easy as that.

Mother Kangaroo watched her little one proudly.
Her pouch was finally empty.
"Don't go too far!" she called,
because Little Kangaroo just kept jumping and jumping.

First published in Belgium and Holland by Clavis Uitgeverij, Hasselt – Amsterdam, 2005
Copyright © 2005, Clavis Uitgeverij

English translation from the Dutch by Clavis Publishing Inc. New York
Copyright © 2017 for the English language edition: Clavis Publishing Inc. New York

Visit us on the web at www.clavisbooks.com

Little Kangaroo written and illustrated by Guido van Genechten
Original title: *Kleine Kangoeroe*
Translated from the Dutch by Clavis Publishing

ISBN 978-1-60537-338-6

This book was printed in February 2017 at Publikum d.o.o., Slavka Rodica 6, Belgrade, Serbia

First Edition
10 9 8 7 6 5 4 3 2 1